P9-BYR-290

In a high-rise building
deep in the heart of a big city
live two private eyes:
Bunny Brown and Jack Jones.
Bunny is the brains,
Jack is the snoop,
and together they
crack cases wide open.

This is the story of
Case Number 006:
THE CASE OF
THE FIDGETY FOX.

story by
Cynthia Rylant

pictures by
G. Brian Karas

THE HIGH-RISE PRIVATE EYES

The High-Rise Private Eyes

The Case of the Fidgety Fox

Greenwillow Books
An Imprint of HarperCollinsPublishers

To Mrs. Dedrick and her eager readers
—G B K

Acrylic, gouache, and pencil were used for the full-color art.
The text type is Times.

Library of Congress Cataloging-in-Publication Data

Rylant, Cynthia.
The high-rise private eyes: the case of the fidgety fox / Cynthia Rylant ;
pictures by G. Brian Karas.
  p.   cm. — (The high-rise private eyes ; 6)
"Greenwillow Books."
Summary: When the fluffy dice of Melvin
the bus driver turn up missing, Bunny and Jack,
two animal detectives, investigate the case.
ISBN 0-06-009101-0 (trade). ISBN 0-06-009102-9 (lib. bdg.)
[1. Animals—Fiction. 2. Dice—Fiction.
3. Mystery and detective stories.]
I. Title: Case of the fidgety fox.
II. Karas, G. Brian, ill. III. Title.
PZ7.R982 Hp 2003   [E]—dc21   2002023532

First Edition 10 9 8 7 6 5 4 3 2 1

Contents

Chapter 1
Cartoons

On Saturday Bunny did her yoga.
Bunny did yoga *every* Saturday.

When she was finished,

she called Jack.

"You're missing all the cartoons,"

Jack said.

"Yes, but I am so very, very calm,"

said Bunny.

"Mighty Monkey is trapped,"

said Jack.

"I'm too calm to care," said Bunny.

"He's in a room full of gardenias,"
said Jack. "And he's allergic."

"Really?" said Bunny.

"That's not good."

"I know," said Jack.

"He's sneezing to high heaven."

"Goodness," said Bunny.

"The Amazing Armadillos
aren't doing too well, either,"
said Jack.

"Really?" said Bunny.

"They're lost in space, and
one of them broke his toe,"
said Jack.

"Gracious, that's not good,"
said Bunny.

"I know," said Jack.

"He wants his mama.

"And Courageous Cat is having
the worst day of all," said Jack.

"Really?" said Bunny.

"He got swallowed by a squid,
and he has to stay there
until next week," said Jack.

"That's awful," said Bunny.

"I know," said Jack. "Stinky, too."

"I don't feel so calm anymore,"
  said Bunny.

"You don't?" asked Jack.

"I feel *trapped*. And *lost*.
  And *swallowed*!" cried Bunny.

"Bunny!" said Jack. "Calm down!"

"I can't," said Bunny.

"You watched too many cartoons."

"I did?" said Jack.

"I need chips," said Bunny.

"Chips calm me down."

"Me, too," said Jack.

"Hurry up and get here!

And bring the ruffly kind!"

Soon Bunny was at Jack's door.

"I have cheesy dip," Jack said.

"Goody," said Bunny.

Bunny and Jack ate lots of chips.

"I'm so calm I can hardly move,"
said Bunny.

"Me, too," said Jack.

"Yoga may be good for you . . ."
said Bunny.

"But it doesn't come
with cheesy dip," finished Jack.

"Right," said Bunny.

"Pass that bowl."

Chapter 2
The Case

Bunny and Jack decided
to take a walk in the park.
"We need the exercise,"
said Bunny,
"after all those chips."
"Right," said Jack.
"Want to get a pretzel
while we're there?"

Bunny and Jack passed the bus stop.
Bus 72 was parked, and its driver
was pacing the sidewalk.
A long line of riders
were waiting to get on.
"Hey!" yelled a beaver.
"I've got to get to the dentist!"

"Let us on the bus!"
  said somebody else.

"Yes, let us on!" cried the others.

"Those guys could use some *chips*,"
  said Jack.

"I wonder why the driver
  won't drive the bus?" said Bunny.

"Well, don't ask him," said Jack.

"I want a nice, salty . . ."

"Sir," said Bunny to the driver,

"why won't you drive the bus?"

"I can't!" said the driver,

   an upset skunk named Melvin.

"I lost my lucky dice!"

"Here, I've got dice," said Jack.

"Take mine."

Bunny looked at Jack.

"Why do you have dice
in your pocket?" asked Bunny.

"For playing backgammon," said Jack.

"But you don't play backgammon,"
said Bunny.

"I play it in my heart," said Jack.

"Oh, for heaven's sake," said Bunny.

"Are you two listening to me?"
  asked Melvin.

"I lost my fluffy dice!"

"Oh," said Jack. "*Fluffy* dice.
  Those are even cooler."

"Do you mean the big dice that
hang from the rearview mirror?"
Bunny asked Melvin.
"Yes," said Melvin.
"I never drive without them."
"And I never eat
without my teeth," said the beaver.
"But I may have to
if you don't get me to the dentist!"

All the other riders in line grumbled.

"A lot of grumbling
going on there," Jack said.

"We really should have brought chips."

Bunny pulled a notepad and pencil
out of her bag.

"A new case?" said Jack.

"Goody!"

Bunny said to Melvin,

"Sir, we are private eyes,
and we can help."

"Now," said Bunny, "when did you
last see your fluffy dice?"
The riders all stopped grumbling
to listen.
"Let's see," said Melvin.
"They were still hanging
on the mirror last night."

"And where did you park the bus?"
  asked Bunny.

"In the bus garage," said Melvin.

"I had a bus garage
  when I was a kid," said Jack.

"Be quiet, Jack," said Bunny.

"It was red," said Jack.

Bunny gave Jack a look.

"But it was very small,"

said Jack.

"*Jack!*" said Bunny.

Bunny turned to Melvin.

"Who else was in the garage?"
   asked Bunny.

"Ed and Teddy," said Melvin.

"Who's Ed?" asked Bunny.

"He's another driver," said Melvin.

"And who's Teddy?" asked Bunny.

"He sweeps the floor,"
   said Melvin.

"We have to make a trip

   to the bus garage tonight,"

   Bunny told Jack.

"Yippee!" said Jack.

"That's no help now!" yelled the beaver.

"Who's going to drive the bus?"

   Everyone looked at Bunny and Jack.

Bunny looked at Jack.

Jack looked at Bunny.

"Well, I do have my lucky dice,"

said Jack.

Melvin handed Jack the keys.

"Break a leg," he said.

"No, don't break *anything*!"

said Bunny as Jack climbed in.

All the riders piled in.

"See you at the bus garage!"
Jack called to Bunny
as he drove off.
"Think *chips*, Jack!" yelled Bunny.
"Think chips!"

At eight o'clock that night
Bunny stood at the door
of the bus garage.

BEEEEEEEP!!! went a loud horn.

"AAAAIIII!!!" screamed Bunny.

She looked behind her.

There was Jack at the wheel

of the empty bus.

"Oops, did I scare you?"

Jack called.

Bunny gave him a look.

"I must have," said Jack.

"You're all white."

"Jack, I'm always all white,"
  said Bunny.
"Oh, all white. Whatever you say,"
  said Jack.
"Ugh," said Bunny.
"Aren't you glad I didn't
  break a leg?" asked Jack.
"I'm glad," said Bunny.
"Now let's solve this case."
"Okey-doke," said Jack.

He climbed off the bus

and stood with Bunny

by the door.

Bunny knocked.

"Anyone there?" she called.

"They're probably in there

telling bus driver tales,"

said Jack.

"Boy, do I have some good ones."

"Concentrate, Jack," said Bunny.

"Like this zebra with the umbrella
    I picked up today," said Jack.
"Later," said Bunny.
"The umbrella had stars on it,"
    said Jack, "so I said . . ."

Suddenly the door opened.

A very large bulldog stood there.

"Yikes," said Jack.

"I'm Ed,"

said the very large bulldog.

"Nice to meet you," said Bunny.

She told Ed about

Melvin's missing fluffy dice.

"I didn't take them," said Ed.

"Of course you didn't," said Jack,

looking up with a very large smile.

"Is that your bus?" Bunny asked Ed,
   pointing to a bus in the garage.

"Yes," said Ed.

"Hmmm," said Bunny,
   looking closely at the bus.
   She made a note in her pad.

"And is Teddy here?" asked Bunny.

"No," said Ed. "He went
   with his grandpa to dance class."

"Teddy's learning to dance?"

asked Bunny.

"No," said Ed.

"Grandpa's learning to dance.

Teddy's learning to drive."

Bunny looked at Jack.

Jack looked at Bunny.

"Bingo!" they both said.

Chapter 4
Solved

Ed told Bunny and Jack

how to get to the dance hall.

They hopped on Jack's bus.

On the way,

they looked over the clues.

"I knew Ed wasn't our man,"
  said Bunny.

"He already has something
  on his mirror."

"What?" asked Jack.

"A little angel," said Bunny.

"You're kidding," said Jack.

"I'm not," said Bunny.

"Ed doesn't look like

an angel kind of guy,"

said Jack.

"Never judge a book by its cover,"

said Bunny.

"I was looking at the book's *teeth*,"

said Jack.

When they got to the dance hall,
Bunny and Jack saw an old Ford
parked out front.
Hanging from its mirror
were fluffy dice.
"Gotcha!" said Jack.

Bunny and Jack went inside.

On the dance floor a very old fox

was learning a trot.

In the corner sat a young fox.

"Are you Teddy?" asked Bunny.

"Yes," said the young fox.

He jumped up
and spilled his pop
on Bunny.

"Oh, sorry," said Teddy.

"Not my lucky day."

"I'll say!" said Bunny.

She told him about

Melvin's fluffy dice.

"Drat," said Teddy.

"Learning to drive?" asked Jack.

"Right," said Teddy.

"Nervous?" asked Jack.

"You bet," said Teddy.

"And you needed Melvin's dice
  for luck," said Bunny.

"Sorry," said Teddy.

"I was going to return them
  after I drove Grandpa home."

"Say," said Jack.

"I've got some little lucky dice.
  Want to trade?"

"Really?" asked the fox.

"Sure," said Jack. "Luck is luck."

  So they swapped.

"Thanks a *lot*!" said Teddy.

"Just tell Melvin you're sorry,

  okay?" said Bunny.

"Sure," Teddy said.

Back at the bus garage,

Jack parked the bus

and left the fluffy dice

on Melvin's mirror.

He and Bunny walked home.

"Do you miss your dice?"

asked Bunny.

"Well, I can't play backgammon

now," said Jack.

"But you never played backgammon,"
said Bunny.

"I played it in my heart," said Jack.

"Oh, for heaven's sake," said Bunny.

"Do you think I've run out of luck
now?" said Jack.

"Not at all," said Bunny.

"You are very lucky."

"Really?" asked Jack.

"Yes," said Bunny.

"You're not trapped with gardenias

  or lost in space

  or swallowed by a squid."

"You're right," said Jack.

"And," said Bunny,

"I bought more chips.

  And cheesy dip."

"Yay!" said Jack. "My lucky day!"